Hannah Moorcroft-ĵ
Illustrated by David Millington

Stinkabell and the Bogsnufflers

Bumblebee Books
London

A CIP catalogue record for this title is
available from the British Library.

ISBN: 978-1-83934-012-3

Bumblebee Books is an imprint of
Olympia Publishers.

First Published in 2021

Bumblebee Books
Tallis House
2 Tallis Street
London
EC4Y 0AB

Printed in Great Britain

www.olympiapublishers.com

Dedication

For my son, Joshua, and for all the children out there who long
for a bit of adventure!

To Erin & Bethany,

I know you're a bit old for this
now but I hope you might enjoy
reading it anyway knowing you
were one of the first to ever hear
about it! Love,
Hannah
xx

CHAPTER 1
THE LAND ON THE OTHER
SIDE OF THE PILLOW

It's sunset in the Land on the Other Side of the Pillow. The Bog Frogs are belching loudly, while the Pongtails swoop wildly back to their grassy nests, their feathers sticking out in all directions after a busy day. Orange Flumpins dip their beaks into the smelly green water, looking for one last snack before bedtime. It's Stinkabell's favourite time of day.

She sits on a little island made of snoggleweed floating in the middle of the bog, dangling her chubby little legs in the dirty water. She loves this place at sunset, watching all the creatures getting ready for bed. There is always a buzz in the air before everything goes quiet for the night.

She spots Lillyplop, her favourite Bog Frog, hopping from clump to clump to get to her. She can always spot Lillyplop, because she has the brightest purple toes of all the frogs in the bog!

With her long tongue, Lillyplop scoops a Dragon Beetle from the air and jumps across to Stinkabell's little island. She belches happily as Stinkabell lovingly strokes her warty back.

The sun is almost gone now and Stinkabell's wings shiver slightly in the chilly air. Her stomach lets out a huge growl. Time to head home for some of mum's delicious Humble-bee pie. Scrumalicious!

"Goodnight, Lillyplop," she says, and flaps her little wings. But just as she is about take-off, something stops her. A sound that makes her bones tingle—a loud, deep, crashing noise, from the other end of the lake. The very ground beneath the bog starts to shake. Waves start breaking against the side of the snoggleweed mound. Suddenly everything goes silent;

the Bog Frogs leap quickly out of sight, the Flumpins change colour from bright orange to snoggleweed-green, making them almost invisible (apart from a pair of beady black eyes, if you should look closely enough).

Stinkabell stands frozen to the spot. She knows this can mean one thing and one thing only: Bogsnufflers!

CHAPTER 2
BOGSNUFFLERS

Bogsnufflers are every bog dweller's worst nightmare. Huge, hideous beasts, that hunt and eat the creatures of the bog. They are like giant, muddy-brown crocodiles, but stand upright. They have sharp yellowy-green spikes along their backs and huge flat feet for crushing their prey. But Bogsnufflers have no teeth, so their long snouts droop like a floppy cucumber. And with no teeth to keep the spit in, they constantly dribble long trails of yellow goo.

If you are ever unlucky enough to get close to one, you'll smell the stink of mouldy bog maggots on its breath, which is extremely unpleasant.

In order to eat their prey, Bogsnufflers need teeth of course. Ordinary teeth like yours and mine. As they don't have their own, they steal these teeth from the Bog Fairies.

They pop the stolen teeth inside their snouts, crunch up whichever poor creature they've chased down and then spit the teeth back out again. Their favourite snacks are juicy Bog Frogs (which taste a bit like fish fingers stuffed with raw chicken). But they also love to feast on Crumpet Slugs, Bat-beetles and pretty much anything their ugly snouts can sniff out in the snoggleweed.

Because their stolen teeth are too small to chew up a bog creature whole, a Bogsnuffler will bite off their poor victim's legs first, and then crunch up their little bones bit by bit, working their way up to the head... You can see why these creatures are not very popular in the Land on the Other Side of the Pillow.

That night when Stinkabell heard the crashing noise from the other side of the bog, she knew she must get home immediately. Not thinking of the danger, she took a running leap and flapped her wings furiously, until she was whizzing over the surface of the water, flying at top speed towards her little white home.

Bog Fairies build their houses from human teeth, which they collect from under human children's pillows in the middle of the night. Teeth make great houses for the fairies. Teeth are strong, warm and waterproof, which is very important to protect the fairies from the ferocious bog storms.

But however solid the houses were, she knew that they were no match for the heavy feet of the Bogsnufflers, who could knock them over with just one kick!

It was a wide patch of bog and it took Stinkabell a hundred wing-flaps to get to the lump of snoggleweed that hid the little row of tooth houses. As she got closer, her heart began pounding faster and faster. She couldn't see it! Where was her home? There was just a sea of green where the little white houses had stood, poking proudly out of the weeds.

She flew until she reached the exact spot where she'd left her house just an hour earlier. She landed on top of the smashed-up tooth rubble and looked round for her parents, shouting their names as loud as she could. But she knew it was no use; she could see all around the flat bog. Every house in the village had disappeared—there was nobody here. It was deserted. The Bogsnuffler had taken all the teeth it could find. But much, much worse, it must have taken the Bog Fairies too.

The Bogsnuffler was nowhere to be seen. Having destroyed the village, it must have made its way to the bog with its stolen teeth to hunt for dinner. Stinkabell thought of poor Lillyplop, hiding out with her family in the muddy water. She just hoped that they were tucked safely away in the snoggleweed and out of the reach of the Bogsnuffler's greedy snout. She couldn't bear to think what would happen to her warty friend if a Bogsnuffler caught her.

CHAPTER 3
TOOTH-TAKING

Stinkabell wiped her tears with her sleeve and tried to think what she should do now. It was bad enough destroying their houses, but she couldn't understand why the Bogsnuffler had taken the Bog Fairies away. She knew it couldn't be to eat them, because Bog Fairies are far too gristly for Bogsnufflers to be able to chew up with the human teeth. So what could it want with her family and friends?

 Stinkabell went back and forth, searching every inch of the snoggleweed around the bog — but with no luck. No one else had managed to escape. She was exhausted, and her wings were soaked through.

The wind was starting to pick up. The Woollyback Squarkers were huddling together for warmth. She could feel in her bones that a bog storm was on its way. There was only one thing to do: Stinkabell would have to rebuild her home herself. But to do that, she needed teeth…

Stinkabell had never collected a tooth from Human Land before and she was terrified. Bog Fairies have a whole term at school to learn about tooth-collecting, and they must pass their TTTs (Tooth-Taking Tests) before they are allowed to set foot in Human Land. But Stinkabell wasn't due to start that until next year. She'd have to remember the stories she'd heard from all the older fairies and hope for the best.

She took a deep breath and lifted her face towards the sky, just like she had seen her parents do so many times before. Then, as best she could remember, she recited the Tooth-Taking Chant out loud:

'Take me high into the night
Far away and out of sight.
Straight through time, faster than light.
Crossing worlds both left and right,
Find me a tooth, smooth and white.'

Her eyes closed tight, hands flattened to her sides, she flew like a dart, straight into the big white cloud that linked the Land on the Other Side of the Pillow with Human Land.

The Connection Cloud felt tingly and soggy. She flapped her wings as fast as she could, and suddenly everything went black and she was spinning round and round, faster and faster, on and on. There was a bright orange flash, and slowing down now she found herself flying through a field of big gold discs. Just in time she reached out and grabbed one and stuffed the heavy coin into the pouch on the front of her dungarees. She'd nearly missed it—that was close!

Next thing she knew, she had stopped spinning and her feet had sunk into something warm and squishy. She blinked her eyes and looked around. Human Land—she'd made it!

But her thrill turned quickly to horror, as Stinkabell realised where she was.

She was standing in a huge room, about a thousand times bigger than her own little room in her white tooth house. Rather than being underneath the pillow, where she would find the tooth and deliver the coin, she was standing on the wrong side of the pillow, the side she was never supposed to see. She had overshot the landing.

Suddenly, she heard a strange snorting noise and, with a jolt, realised she wasn't alone. Hot breath ruffled her wings, making her shudder from toe to nose. She didn't need to turn to know there was a real-life child in the bed, with its head right beside her on the pillow!

She turned as slowly as she could, hoping to sneak back under the pillow, but as she turned she saw the human child looking right at her with wide eyes. The hairs on her toes stood on end and she froze.

Then it spoke. 'You're the Tooth Fairy!'

'I'm not! I'm a Bog Fairy!' she replied. But as soon as she'd spoken, Stinkabell realised the awful thing she'd done. Humans don't know about Bog Fairies; it's the best kept secret in history. Now she had changed that forever.

'Oh. So—if you're not the Tooth Fairy, then why are you here?' asked the child, with a confused frown. Stinkabell paused for a second and wondered whether she could make a run for the pillow, but the child seemed so huge she decided that she was going to have to trust it and hope for the best.

'I came to collect your tooth,' she said.

'Ah ha! Then you are the Tooth Fairy—' said the child, sitting up gleefully, '—that's what we call you anyway. But I didn't think you'd look like… this…' it said.

Stinkabell looked down at her flat, hairy, webbed feet and dirty dungarees. Apart from her curly orange hair, which she could tell was sticking out all over the place after the flight, she looked just the same as usual. What did the human expect her to look like?

She took a closer look at the child. It wasn't exactly what she'd imagined either. It was very large, with smooth brown skin, short curly black hair and big, sparkly brown eyes. Stinkabell decided, from what she'd heard about human beings, that this was most likely a boy child.

'I'm Stinkabell,' she said, pulling herself up to her full height (she was about two caterpillars tall, one of the tallest in her class). The boy laughed out loud, but he quickly stopped laughing when he saw Stinkabell's hurt expression.

'Sorry,' he said, 'that's a very… interesting name.'

Stinkabell continued, 'Maybe you humans call us Tooth Fairies, but in our world we're just Bog Fairies.'

'Woah, you're from another world?' said the boy, his eyes wide. 'Where is it? How did you get here? Is it the same as Earth?'

'It's just on the other side of the pillow,' said Stinkabell. 'I flew into the Connection Cloud as fast as I could, and then everything went dark and I popped out here. But you're not supposed to see me. I've never done this before and I've really messed up,' she said sadly, her wings drooping miserably behind her.

'I'm Dillon,' said the boy, 'I didn't mean to see you, but something hit my head and it woke me up. Why have you messed everything up?'

Before she knew it, Stinkabell had told Dillon the whole story. She told him about the bog creatures and her tooth house on the edge of the bog. She even told him all about the guzzling Bogsnuffler and what it had done to her village, and to her parents. Dillon sat and listened while she talked, staring at her with his mouth hanging open.

When she finished, he smacked his hand on the pillow, sending Stinkabell flying into the air, and growled, 'This is totally crazy! How can those murdering, tooth-stealing Bogsnufflers get away with it? Someone's got to stop them.'

With that, he jumped out of bed and ran over to the little desk in the corner of his room. 'Right, come on Stinkabell,' he said, 'we need to make a plan. We're going to find out what the Bogsnufflers are doing with the fairies. But first we need to figure out how to get you some teeth to rebuild your house.'

He dashed back to his bed, lifted up the pillow, and pulled out the smooth white tooth that he'd placed there so carefully before he went to sleep. 'Here, this is a big one,' he said proudly.

'Wow, thanks!' said Stinkabell, examining the tooth. 'Great start! And this is for you.' She took the coin from the pouch in her dungarees and handed it to Dillon.

Dillon looked delighted and put the coin in his pocket. Then he stuck his finger in his mouth and started tugging his back teeth.

'No other wobbly ones, I'm afraid; I've lost pretty much all of mine already. We'll have to think of something else.'

Suddenly Dillon's eyes sparkled, and he grinned from ear to ear.

'I know!' he said 'Of course. The place where there are enough teeth to build a palace—the dentist!'

'The whatist?' asked Stinkabell, confused.

'It's like a hospital,' Dillon explained, 'but people go to there have their teeth checked. The dentist sometimes has to take out rotten teeth— my Mum had one out last week. If I tell Mum I have a toothache, she'll make me an appointment to see the dentist. I'll take you with me in my backpack and while we're there you can sneak in and take some of the old teeth. It's genius!' he cried, doing a little victory dance in the middle of the floor.

Stinkabell couldn't help but smile too. Dillon's happiness was catching and it did sound like a great plan—just imagine, a place where there are enough teeth to build a palace!

CHAPTER 4
THE DENTIST

Dillon and Stinkabell spent the rest of the night carefully planning their trip, until they had everything worked out. As the sun began to shine through his window, Dillon slid Stinkabell in his pyjama pocket and got back into bed. A few minutes later, Dillon's mum came in to wake him for school as usual.

'Owwwwww,' Dillon groaned dramatically, holding his jaw. 'My mouth hurts, Mum.'

'Oh no,' said the voice of someone Stinkabell couldn't see 'do you have a sore tooth?'

'Yes, I've been awake for HOURS,' he whimpered (well that bit was true, anyway, and although he felt guilty for fooling his mum—he had to help his new friend and this was the only way).

'OK, I'll call the dentist and tell them it's an emergency,' she sighed.

An hour later, Stinkabell was whizzing along in a car for the first time. It was much quicker than flying, but she did miss the feeling of the wind between her wings. She was inside Dillon's backpack and couldn't see a thing, so she spent the journey going through the plan in her head. She had no idea what a dentist would be like. I'm sure they're lovely humans, just like Dillon, she thought.

But she couldn't have been more wrong. Dr McAvity (as she insisted on being called, though she wasn't actually a doctor at all) was one of those people who was born miserable. She was tall and thin, with mousy hair scraped back into a tiny bun on top of her head. Her skin was white, and her white dentist coat sat over a pair of white trousers, capped by white shoes. She wore no jewellery and no make up; McAvity was colourless in every way.

'She probably became a dentist because she enjoyed doing nasty things to other people,' Dillon whispered, opening up his backpack flap so Stinkabell could see. Dr McAvity glared in Dillon's direction and then strode out of the waiting room, with her next victim following nervously behind her.

Dillon and his mum were now the only people in the waiting room. The plan could commence! Dillon strolled casually over to the table of books and magazines.

'Mum, do you want to read "House and Home"?' he said sweetly. His mum looked a little surprised but accepted the offer, and Dillon delivered a crinkled-up copy of the magazine to her with a big smile. As soon as she was distracted behind the pages, he tipped Stinkabell out onto the floor.

Stinkabell shook herself and tried to get her bearings. She winked at Dillon, and tiptoed to the door through which the dentist had left the room. Squeezing through the small gap, she found herself in a long corridor with several doors coming off it. Stinkabell remembered Dillon's instructions. She pressed her ear to the first door and listened. A loud buzzing sound was coming from inside. She moved quickly to the next one. Just as she was about to lean in to listen, the door opened and the child she'd seen earlier came out, sniffing and holding his hand to his mouth. He left a trail of red drool behind him as he walked back to the waiting room. Stinkabell started to wonder what she'd got herself into, but she shook herself, flapped her wings and fluttered in through the door, landing on a cupboard in the corner of the room.

She looked around. The dentist's surgery was nothing like she imagined. Everything was so bright and shiny; it hurt her eyes. And the walls didn't seem to be made of teeth, like she'd assumed they would be. There were glass bottles filled with coloured liquids on shelves all around the room. Dr McAvity sat on a stool, holding something up to the light. Stinkabell squinted to see it, and realised it was a small tooth.

'Good work Mabel, we've got another one,' she said with a smirk, to a small, round lady wearing a blue apron. Mabel picked up a huge jar and carried it over to McAvity, who happily popped the tooth inside with a clink.

The jar was at least three quarters full of small white teeth.

'Did that boy really need his tooth taking out?' Mabel asked, timidly.

'Of course not, but when did I ever let that stop me?' snapped McAvity. 'It's pay day today, Mabel, and those snivelling kids' teeth are going to make our fortune!

We've got until five o'clock to grab ourselves a few more before the collection.' She glanced at the clock on the wall. 'The Bogsnuffler won't come until it's dark; we'll meet outside at the back of the surgery so we won't be seen.'

Stinkabell jumped in complete surprise—she couldn't believe what she was hearing. She had to work so hard to stop herself from gasping out loud, that wisps of steam hissed from her ears with the effort. How could a Bogsnuffler be here in Human Land?

McAvity walked to the door, saying to Mabel over her shoulder, 'I'll fetch the next one. I had a look at him when he came in—lovely white teeth. I think I'll take two!' She gave a nasty throaty chuckle and headed for the door.

Stinkabell had to stop her—or Dillon would be next!

CHAPTER 5
THE GREAT ESCAPE

Stinkabell kept close behind the crazy dentist as she stalked down the corridor. Dillon was sitting opposite the door, and looked up as McAvity walked in. Stinkabell had to get his attention, but she would have to distract the dentist first. Using all her energy, she flew straight into the back of the white dentist's coat. McAvity stopped, straightened up, and flicked her hand behind her back to see what had hit her. Stinkabell darted to the side to avoid the long fingers, then flew at her again. This time the dentist span right round to see what was there. But Stinkabell was too quick and flew round behind her so she stayed out of sight. As she flew around the dentist, she saw Dillon watching with some confusion. When he saw Stinkabell, he put his hand over his mouth to cover up a giggle. Stinkabell pointed at the door, to try and make Dillon understand that he had to get out of there.

McAvity was grunting with frustration now, spinning round and batting the air behind her with both hands, while Stinkabell, who was quite enjoying herself, kept flying at her from different directions. Dillon grabbed his mum's arm and pulled her to the door.

'Mum, I think we should come back later.'

By now Dillon's mum had no intention of letting this woman near her son. 'Yes, I think that's probably for the best,' she muttered, hurrying out of the front door behind Dillon. Stinkabell dashed for the closing door, her wings skimming through by a millimetre just as it swung shut.

As McAvity continued swatting wildly at the air, hissing in anger that she couldn't catch her invisible attacker, Stinkabell caught a glimpse of Mabel watching the unexpected scene through the door. She had a distinct smile on her face.

In the car on the way home, Dillon lifted Stinkabell out of his backpack onto his shoulder.

'What happened? Did you get the teeth?' he hissed.

'No,' Stinkabell whispered urgently, 'she's collecting the children's teeth to sell them to the Bogsnufflers.'

'No way!' Dillon cried out loud in shock.

'What is it, Dillon?' asked his mum from the front of the car

'Umm… I'm just saying that dentist was really scary, Mum, can we find a new one?'

'I suppose we should, she's certainly a strange woman,' said Dillon's mum. She turned up the radio and starting humming along.

'She's meeting the Bogsnufflers tonight,' Stinkabell whispered into Dillon's ear. 'She's got a huge jar of teeth and she said they would pay her for them.'

'Blimey,' said Dillon, 'this is so messed up! We'll have to sneak back there tonight and watch what happens.'

Later that evening, Stinkabell curled up on Dillon's bed while he ate dinner downstairs with his mum. She had only been in Human Land for a day but her head spun with what had already happened. There was so much to take in: new sights, new sounds, new smells. And so many people! Back in the bog it was always the same view—green snoggleweed, greeny-brown water, the odd white tooth house peeking out from behind some tall weeds. Here, there was something new around every corner. She needed to keep her wits about her!

The door opened and Dillon bounced into the room.

'I brought you this,' he said proudly, and handed Stinkabell a strange bumpy brown disc. 'It's a chocolate biscuit,' said Dillon seeing her confused expression. 'I wasn't sure what you normally eat?'

'Humble-bees, usually,' said Stinkabell, 'or Pongtail eggs. Sometimes Mum makes snoggleweed mash, but that's disgusting!' A sadness fell over Stinkabell's little face when she thought of her mum and that she may never see her again, and a big tear plopped onto the pillow.

'You must really miss them,' said Dillon quietly. He broke off a small piece of the biscuit and pushed it towards her. 'Here, try this, it might cheer you up a bit. Then we'll go and find a way to stop those Bogsnufflers, so they'll never hurt an innocent creature again.'

Stinkabell sniffed loudly and wiped her face. She was starving, so she picked up the piece of lumpy brown stuff and had a little sniff. Her wings tingled slightly as she nibbled cautiously at the edge, then they clapped together in sheer delight. It was the most delicious thing she'd ever eaten! Crumbs flew everywhere, as she stuffed the wonderful brown goodness into her little mouth.

Dillon watched with delight as Stinkabell gobbled the whole biscuit (which was nearly as big as her) and then buzzed happily around his bed, sucking up stray crumbs.

'You remind me of a bumblebee,' he laughed.

Stinkabell straightened up. 'I think you mean a Humble-bee,' she said in a matter-of-fact voice. 'I'm nothing like a Humble-bee; for a start I'm a kind of pinky colour, not see-through, and I can't fly at a hundred flaps a minute... and I only have two eyes, like you.'

'Oh,' said Dillon, 'I've never heard of a Humble-bee, but they don't sound anything like our bumblebees. Ours are round and furry. They buzz when they fly like you do and they have the same shaped wings.'

Stinkabell sighed. Despite everything, she missed her boggy home— the belching of the Bog Frogs, the humming of the Dragon Beetles and the far-off cry of the Woollyback Squarkers. Everything was topsy-turvy in Human Land!

The sun had finally disappeared and a dark grey had fallen over the road outside. It was time to go. Dillon lifted Stinkabell into his backpack and put it on. Now was the tricky bit. He knew his mum would be in the living room. She'd be lying on the sofa with her feet up, watching one of her boring programmes.

As quietly as he could, Dillon pulled the door open and crept onto the landing. He had to pass the living room to get to the kitchen, where he could sneak out of the back door. The stairs were easy; Dillon knew the creaky ones, so each time he reached one, he grabbed the bannisters with both hands and swung himself over without putting his feet down.

At the bottom of the stairs the living room door was open a crack, so Dillon dropped to the floor and shuffled past on his hands and knees, in case his mum looked over and saw him. He was wearing his jacket, backpack and trainers, which would be sure to give them away if he got caught.

But they got past with no alerts and as Dillon pulled the back door shut behind him, he let out a huge sigh of relief, grabbed his bike from the wall, and started pedalling as fast as he could down the road.

They had to hurry. Between the streetlights it was almost dark, and they had to take several roads to get to the dentist's surgery. Everything was much quieter now. Stinkabell could hear a few cars passing by, muffled through the backpack. Otherwise, all was still.

CHAPTER 6
THE EXCHANGE

Dillon ditched his bike behind the wall at the front of the surgery, and crept as quietly as he could down the little alley which led to the back of the building. He couldn't see much and nearly went flying when he tripped over a stinky bin bag. At the back of the building, Dillon stopped. There was a small concrete yard, surrounded by thick trees. They couldn't step out into the yard or they'd be seen. They would have to stay here, and peek their heads round the wall to see what was happening. It was quiet and the only light shone from a room inside the surgery. Dillon slid off his backpack to let Stinkabell out. Now all they had to do was wait.

After what felt like forever, Stinkabell heard a noise. It was very faint but she knew the sound—a deep crashing in the distance. Her wings shuddered. She flew onto Dillon's shoulder and whispered, 'It's coming.'

Dillon got into position, so he could watch the action from the safety of the alley. There was a crash from the other side of the trees and the ground began to shake. Dillon and Stinkabell looked at each other; her heart was racing and she could tell that Dillon was nervous too.

Then, just to their left, a tall tree fell with a loud thump across the yard. A huge flat scaly foot came into view. Dillon and Stinkabell ducked further back into the alley, as a huge, looming dark shape crossed in front of them into the yard. Stinkabell held her breath.

There was a clunk from the surgery as a door opened and light flooded the yard. Stinkabell and Dillon cautiously poked their heads around the corner. Dillon gasped as he saw the strange creature for the first time.

'It's a real-life monster,' he stammered, not taking his eyes off the weirdest beast he'd ever seen. Stinkabell nodded. It was the closest she'd ever been to a Bogsnuffler. She could detect the familiar smell of snoggleweed and something else, that could have been mouldy bog maggots.

From their hiding place it was difficult to hear what was going on, so Stinkabell carefully crept into the yard, keeping close to the wall to make sure she wouldn't be seen. The Bogsnuffler had his back to her, but now she could see McAvity standing tall in the doorway, and behind her shoulder, a glimpse of Mabel's curly hair. McAvity held out the giant jar of teeth to the Bogsnuffler, who grabbed it and held it up to the light. He gave the jar a good shake, then with one long scaly claw opened it, fished out some teeth, and popped them one by one in his gummy mouth.

With the teeth in place the droopy snout stood out straight like a crocodile's. The Bogsnuffler gave an odd grin, showing off a line of small white teeth stuck into the green slimy gums.

Satisfied with its new teeth, it held out a small brown bag that Stinkabell hadn't noticed before. The bag was bulging and moving, as if there was something alive inside. Stinkabell edged forward for a better view. McAvity took the bag and carefully opened it. As she did so, something flew out of the top and straight into the dentist's face! It was the size of three caterpillars with long bee-like wings. Stinkabell nearly fainted from shock. It was a Bog Fairy!

McAvity grabbed the fairy, squishing it in her bony fist, and pushed it back inside the bag. Giving a little nod, she said, 'Same time on Tuesday,' and the exchange was over.

The Bogsnuffler turned and crashed its way back into the trees, clutching the jar of teeth. Back to the Land on the Other Side of the Pillow, to find some poor, terrified bog creatures to crunch with its stolen gnashers, Stinkabell thought sadly.

McAvity spoke urgently. 'Mabel, fetch the jars. We need to lock these fairies away so they can't escape.'

Mabel didn't move straight away, though. Instead she said in a small, quiet voice, 'What will happen to the fairies? What will those people DO to them?'

McAvity smirked and said, 'Some people believe that fairies have magical properties that make humans look younger. They grind up their bones in a power and put them in face cream. People pay a fortune for it. Why do you care anyway? We'll just take the money and forget about them.' She held up the bag, gave it a prod with a long, white, skinny finger, and walked back inside.

Stinkabell could hardly breathe. Her wings were shaking with rage. She HAD to do something to get those Bog Fairies away from the evil dentist. With no plan, Stinkabell started to fly towards the door. But almost immediately, she came to a dead stop in mid-air. Looking round, she realised that Dillon had grabbed hold of her legs.

'Let go of me,' she said, struggling to get her legs free. 'I have to help them Dillon. My mum and dad could be in that bag.'

'I know!' hissed Dillon, 'but you can't just fly straight in there— they'll see you and put you in a jar with the others! We've got to be clever and come up with a plan.'

CHAPTER 7
THE PLAN

Half an hour later they were sitting at the little desk in Dillon's room. Dillon had a pen and notebook ready, so they could write down their plan.

'So, this is what we know: Dr McAvity is stealing teeth from her patients and giving them to the Bogsnufflers, in exchange for Bog Fairies.' Stinkabell nodded sadly. Dillon continued, 'She sells the fairies for loads of money to some secret company who crush up their bones to put in face creams.' Stinkabell swallowed at this awful thought, and nodded again.

'And in the Land on the Other Side of the Pillow the Bogsnufflers are stealing fairies from their homes. Then they're bringing them here to change them for children's teeth, which they need so they can eat the bog creatures?' Stinkabell nodded once more.

'Wow. This is the craziest thing I've ever heard!' Dillon said shaking his head slowly. 'The next exchange is on Tuesday, which gives us less than five days to figure out how to stop the dentist AND the Bogsnufflers.'

'And rescue my parents and the other Bog Fairies,' added Stinkabell.

'There's no way we can do it!' said Dillon, dropping the pen. 'We need help.'

'No!' Stinkabell pleaded. 'We CAN'T tell anyone else. You're not even supposed to have seen me.'

Dillon leant down and looked at her kindly. 'I get it Stinkabell, but this is serious. I'm only a kid—I can't help them on my own. You have to trust me.'

Stinkabell thought about how much Dillon had helped her up until now. If it wasn't for him, she wouldn't have known about the captured Bog Fairies. She definitely couldn't do this alone.

'OK Dillon, I trust you,' she said, still a bit worried inside.

The next morning, Stinkabell and Dillon waited for his mum to

COLOUR
Eat bog Creatures!
COLOUR
Kids Teeth
Bog fairies
Loads of Money!
£
Cream
Fairy bones
face cream
RULER

come and wake him up. Stinkabell hid behind the pillow trying to resist the urge to peek. She heard Dillon's mum open the door and say, 'How are you this morning, poppet? Is the tooth better?'

'Mum,' said Dillon, in a serious voice, 'I've got to tell you something. It's going to sound pretty weird, but it's all true, okay?'

'OK, tell me what is it, Dillon,' she said, sitting down on the bed, which made it wobble so much that Stinkabell nearly toppled over.

Dillon told his mum the whole story of meeting Stinkabell, the Land on the Other Side of the Pillow, and what they had discovered at the dentist.

Stinkabell couldn't see anything from her hiding place so she had no idea what Dillon's mum was thinking as she listened. They had agreed that Stinkabell would come out from her hiding place once Dillon got to the end of the story. But at the very moment she was about to reveal herself, Dillon's mum stood up and said, 'I'm calling the doctor Dillon. Your tooth infection has given you some very wild dreams. We'll get you some medicine and you'll feel much better soon. Stay in your bed; no school today!' Stinkabell heard her hurry out of the room and down the stairs to call the doctor.

'Aaaarggghhhh!' shouted Dillon as loudly as he could, with his face buried in the pillow. The noise startled Stinkabell, who peeked her curly head out to see what caused it.

Dillon's cheeks were a dark red colour, and his usually happy face was all screwed up. 'She thinks I made it up!' he howled. He banged his fists down hard on the duvet then pulled it right up over his head.

Stinkabell crept over and tried to lift a corner of the duvet.

'Dillon...' she whispered. There was no response, so she tried again. This time Dillon rolled over, so he was facing away from Stinkabell.

'That's it then. There's nothing we can do. You'll have to go back to the Land on the Other Side of the Pillow and forget about everything,' he said, without turning around.

Stinkabell's tummy twisted up like she'd eaten a bad caterpillar. She couldn't believe Dillon was giving up. She NEEDED him. As she sat on the pillow, tears started pouring down her pink cheeks. She couldn't bear to go back to the bog without her parents and friends, knowing she could be taken by a Bogsnuffler at any time and end up locked in a jar.

'We can't give up,' she whispered through her tears. 'I can't just go home and let those poor Bog Fairies be tortured by human beings. Once they find how to make money from us, they'll hunt us more and more, and eventually there won't be any Bog Fairies left at all.'

Dillon didn't say anything, and Stinkabell's heart sank. She started to lose hope and, even worse, she worried that she'd lost her new friend.

But then Dillon rolled slowly back over to face Stinkabell. After a long look, he finally said, 'I was wrong. There's never nothing we can do. If we believe in something enough, then we have to fight for it, however impossible it seems.' He reached out a finger to Stinkabell, and she wrapped her little hand around it. A big smile spread across her face and she gave a huge sniff.

'Thank you, Dillon,' she whispered, 'you're the best friend I've ever had.'

CHAPTER 8
THE POTION

Dillon didn't fancy a trip to the doctor, so he managed to convince his mum that he was feeling better and just had a funny turn.

'Of course the fairy story was ridiculous! Yes, it must all have been a weird dream…' But now he couldn't stay home from school, so Stinkabell found herself back inside the backpack, whizzing along on the back seat of the car.

School in Human Land was the craziest place that Stinkabell had ever been! As soon as they were settled in class, (it was science class, Dillon told her) she poked her head out of the flap of the backpack. Everywhere she looked were pairs of children's legs.

It couldn't be more different from her own school (South Bog Primary). There she learned advanced flying, how to build with teeth, bog swimming (the worst), and next year she would be taking the most important class of all: tooth-taking.

Her school was built on a huge snoggleweed island and could be seen for miles around, with its two huge teeth towers. They sat at tooth desks on small tooth stools, facing the toothboard (made from rotten teeth that had gone black). Even the toilets were teeth with holes in them. This school was not like South Bog Primary in any way.

Here there were so many colours; a rainbow of bags, coats, books, posters, pens, even the socks she saw poking from the bottom of the children's trousers.

It sounded different too. Instead of the low buzzing of wings, there was the thumping of feet and scuffing of chairs and chattering from all around. It was hectic and crazy and Stinkabell loved it!

Excited to see more of the classroom, Stinkabell squeezed herself out of Dillon's bag and fluttered up to sit on the empty chair next to him. She couldn't be seen by the other children or the teacher, but now she could see what was going on above her. On each table, there was a plastic bottle. The children were putting white powder in the bottle, and then pouring in a mixture of coloured liquids.

She had to duck quickly under the desk when the teacher (Mr Preacher) suddenly appeared, poking his long nose over Dillon's table, to make sure they were doing the experiment right. With his shiny bald head, and small bulging eyes behind a pair of huge plastic glasses, he looked a bit like a Woollyback Squarker. He stood beadily, watching the children pour each ingredient into the bottle. He nodded his polished head and walked to the next table.

What Stinkabell saw next almost made her little fairy brain bubble over! A frothy white liquid exploded out of the top of the bottle and ran fizzing and floating down the sides. It looked like white lava bursting from the top of a volcano. Stinkabell giggled in delight as she watched the bottles exploding all around her. And suddenly, she had an idea.

Back home after a long and exciting school day, Stinkabell told Dillon her plan.

'We can make our own lava, just like you did today. Then we'll get the Bogsnufflers to eat it!' Dillon looked blankly at Stinkabell, so she pressed on. 'Just think what it would do to them; if we gave them enough it would bubble up in their bellies and make lava pour out of their snouts... they'd be so frightened, they'd run a mile!'

'Yeah, maybe they'd actually explode from the inside! That would be pretty cool,' said Dillon, catching on, 'but how will we get them to eat it?' Stinkabell beamed at him. She knew what they had to do. Although it would be dangerous, she had a feeling it might just work!

Stinkabell and Dillon spent the weekend hatching their plan. They had to work out every detail; there was no room for things to go wrong, or Stinkabell would end up in a science lab.

Dillon had agreed to sneak back to the science cupboard at lunchtime, to get ingredients for the lava. He hoped the teacher would be busy in the playground. Stinkabell wanted some extra ingredients for good measure. She suggested snoggleweed or a Snig-feather, but as those aren't so easy to get hold of in Human Land, Dillon said he would grab what he could and hope for the best.

Stinkabell had to stay at home, as Dillon worried she might get squashed by all the ingredients he had to fit inside his backpack. She was desperate to know how the raid had gone. She fluttered around his room, and tried to distract herself by making faces in front of the shiny round glass thing. As soon as she heard Dillon's voice downstairs, she flew to the door.

Straight away, she knew Dillon had pulled it off. She could see the excitement in his big brown eyes. He opened his bag and pulled out the magic ingredients, announcing each one as he placed it on the table:
- Baking soda (white powder – three tubs)
- Vinegar (brown liquid – one giant bottle)
- A bottle of washing up liquid (for added bubbliness)

- Some white chalk dust (to make the mixture the colour of teeth)
- Finally, some popping candy (that he swapped with a girl at school for a packet of Hoola Hoops) for an extra helping of POP!

Stinkabell was so excited that she swooped around the room in circles. Dillon poured as much of the dry ingredients as he could fit into a small plastic bottle, just small enough to strap onto Stinkabell's back. Then he poured the vinegar, and a drop or two of washing-up liquid into one of the water balloons he was keeping for the next water fight they had in the park.

Now they had to wait till the following evening, when the next exchange was set to take place.

CHAPTER 9
THE FINAL SHOWDOWN

The sky was grey and gloomy when Stinkabell and Dillon arrived back at the dentist surgery. Dillon let Stinkabell out at the back door and tied a bottle that contained all the potion ingredients (except for the vinegar, which would have to be added at the last moment to make the lava explode) to her back, so that it sat like a little backpack between her wings. Stinkabell took a few steps and did a little wiggle, to check the bottle was secure. Dillon gave her a small nod and ruffled her wild hair to say good luck—it was show time.

Stinkabell crept inside the open doorway, being careful to stay in the shadows. Although she was strong, the bottle was big and too heavy for her to fly with, so she had to tiptoe down the hall, trying very hard not to spill any of the potion as she went.

She pushed open the door to McAvity's room and flapped her wings in relief to see that it was empty. The jar of teeth was on the side, in the same spot as before. She just had to get to it. She climbed carefully up onto the huge black chair. Just as Dillon had said, there were two buttons on the arm of the chair. Stinkabell picked one and pushed down on it with all her strength. The chair, very slowly, started to move downwards. It was the wrong button! She quickly pushed the other button and after what seemed an age, the seat began to move slowly upwards… towards the worktop where the tooth jar sat. Higher and higher she went, until finally she was level with the jar. But just at that moment, the door flew open with a loud bang.

Stinkabell held her breath. She glanced round, expecting to see the bony white body of Dr McAvity towering above her. What she saw instead was Mabel, in her blue apron, standing in the doorway, looking right at her. Mabel didn't move; she just stood in the doorway, staring at Stinkabell, as if she was frozen to the spot.

Then a voice broke the silence. McAvity's voice, somewhere behind her in the darkness, 'Mabel, hurry up and get the jar.'

Stinkabell couldn't hide and she couldn't run; she was trapped. She was going to have her bones crushed and put into a face cream. She squeezed her eyes shut as Mabel started crossing the room, heading straight for her. She felt a warm hand scoop her up and heard herself squeak as she was lifted into the air. Then she stopped moving.

Cautiously, Stinkabell opened one eye and saw that she was on Mabel's open hand hovering above the jar of teeth. Then, to her amazement, Mabel gave her a little tip, so that the potion spilled out from the bottle, straight into the open jar of teeth.

Once it was empty, Mabel closed one hand around Stinkabell and picked up the jar of teeth in the other, then hurried towards the door.

On reaching the courtyard, where McAvity was waiting she gingerly handed over the jar of teeth, now mixed with the white lava potion. McAvity grabbed it out of her hands, tutting, 'About time, Mabel.'

Mabel muttered an apology and bent down as if she was tying up her shoelace, but instead she dropped Stinkabell carefully onto the ground by her foot.

Stinkabell shook herself down, relieved to be free, and ran to the alley, keeping to the dark shadows so she was hidden from the beady eyes of McAvity.

No sooner had Stinkabell had crept back to where Dillon was hiding, than they heard the familiar deep groan and felt the ground begin to shudder. She didn't have time to tell Dillon the whole story, so she gave him a thumbs-up, pointing at the jar in Mabel's hand. He handed her the vinegar-filled water balloon. It wobbled around, and she had to squeeze it tightly in her little hands to keep a grip on it.

After a couple of minutes, the long, droopy snout appeared through the trees, followed by the big, flat feet and fat, scaly belly.

Stinkabell squeezed her eyes shut; she was so worried that the plan wouldn't work that she couldn't bear to watch. Was the potion strong enough? What if the Bogsnuffler decided not to test the teeth in its snout this time?

Stinkabell heard McAvity saying, 'Right, let's get on with this.' She must have handed over the jar, because there was a loud sloshing noise of the teeth being shaken around against the glass. This was it, the moment of truth.

Stinkabell flattened herself against the wall, and peered very carefully around the corner to see what was happening. As she did, she saw that the Bogsnuffler was opening up his long snout ready to pop in a row of pearly whites.

This was her cue. Stinkabell sprang into action; she flew silently up behind the Bogsnuffler, clutching the water balloon like her life depended on it. (Well, it probably did!) When its mouth was as wide open as it would go, she flew over the top of its head so she was directly on top of the gaping, gummy snout.

From up there she could see straight into the huge slimy brown throat, and she couldn't help thinking how terrible it would be if that was the last thing you ever saw. But there was no time for thinking—she had to act, and she had to act now!

She swooped down and dropped the balloon straight into the wide-open mouth. As the balloon disappeared down the Bogsnuffler's throat, Stinkabell flapped her wings as hard as she could to get out of the way of the now tooth-filled jaws, before they could snap shut with her inside!

CHAPTER 10
THE ERUPTION

For a couple of seconds, nothing happened at all. Then came the fireworks! When the balloon burst in the Bogsnuffler's snout and the vinegar mixed with the potion on the teeth, it caused dozens of noisy little explosions in the Bogsnuffler's mouth. The foam forced the Bogsuffler's snout back open and great streams of it burst out, like white lava from a brown, scaly volcano. More and more lava poured out, until they could hardly see the creature beneath!

Stinkabell watched the incredible scene from Dillon's shoulder. Neither said a word; they just stared in amazement, waiting to see what would happen next.

The Bogsnuffler started to spin round and round like a clockwork toy, slowly at first but quickly gathering pace, first in one direction, then the other. The lava kept coming, and it got even fizzier as the popping candy kicked in and started little eruptions inside the Bogsnuffler's stomach.

The creature started wheezing very loudly and blowing clouds of white foam from its snout. Stinkabell and Dillon watched with delight as it started to run towards the woods, as fast as its clumsy feet would carry it. It stumbled and steamed as it went, it was quite a sight!

Eventually, it disappeared from view, but puffs of foam could still be seen shooting into the sky over the tree tops in the distance, and a nasty smell of mouldy snoggleweed mixed with rotting fish bones lingered in the air.

Stinkabell turned to look at McAvity's face. Her eyes remained fixed on the woods, while her face twisted into a mixture of disgust and disbelief. The eyes boggled, the nostrils flared and the lips stretched into a snarl, showing her clenched teeth.

Catching sight of Stinkabell, Mabel swung into action. She spun round to face McAvity.

'Give me the bag,' she said calmly, but with a new sense of authority. McAvity snapped out of her trance and looked at Mabel with a confused frown.

'What are you talking about?' she barked.

'It's not right what we've been doing,' said Mabel, standing her ground. 'I won't let you hand those poor fairies over to be chopped into pieces. And I won't stand by and watch you pull healthy children's teeth out ever again.' By now, Mabel was on a roll; it was the first time she'd ever stood up to McAvity. She continued: 'I should have stopped this as soon as I found out what was going on, but I was too scared of you. Well, not anymore. I'm calling the police right now and turning you in'.

'They'll never believe you,' sneered McAvity, 'it's your word against mine and I'M A DOCTOR!'

Suddenly, Dillon stepped forward into the light. 'No it's not,' he said. 'It's our word against yours. I saw the whole thing.'

Stinkabell watched the dentist's face fill with rage. The next thing she knew, McAvity was charging right at them. For a second, Stinkabell thought she was going for Dillon—but then she ran straight past them, heading for the trees. She was trying to run away!

'Quick!' yelled Stinkabell. 'Grab her!'

Dillon turned to chase the fleeing dentist but before he could move, Mabel bounded past them and, with a strange yelp, took a giant leap into the air. She landed right on the dentist's back, knocking her to the ground with a crash. McAvity howled as she fell. She thrashed around, trying to get free, but Mabel spread out her arms and legs like a star, pinning her prisoner to the ground.

'What are you planning to do now then, Mabel?' came a muffled snarl, through the pile on the floor.

'I'm going to call the police,' said Mabel. 'Something I should have done a long time ago.'

'Noooo!' Stinkabell shouted to Mabel. 'You can't call the police. No one else can know about us.' She flew to where Mabel was lying in a heap of limbs. 'Please?' She looked Mabel in the eyes so she'd see how serious she was.

'It's OK,' said Mabel, 'I'm not going to tell anyone about you. All I need to say is that Dr McAvity has been pulling out children's healthy teeth, for no reason other than for her own amusement. I've got all the proof I need in the office.'

'Ha!' laughed McAvity. 'I think you're forgetting that you helped me take those teeth, Mabel. You were my assistant. They'll punish you too!'

Mabel slumped and gave a deep sigh. Stinkabell thought she might change her mind and set the dentist free. But then she spoke in a calm voice.

'I know. I'm so ashamed of what I did. I deserve to be punished too. I'm not going to pretend that I didn't play a part.' She wriggled a phone out from her pocket whilst still pinning McAvity down, and called the police. She told them everything (well, everything except the bit about the Bog Fairies and the Bogsnufflers, much to Stinkabell's relief).

Once she had made the call and the police were on their way to the surgery, Mabel and Dillon grabbed one of the dentist's arms each and pulled her to her feet.

McAvity was done fighting; she looked deflated (and a little squashed). She stood quietly while they waited for the police. And it wasn't long before they heard the sirens in the distance.

Stinkabell watched from the alley as the police dragged McAvity to a big car with a blue flashing light. Mabel took the police into the dentist surgery, and showed them all the evidence they needed to lock McAvity up.

Stinkabell heard the police tell Mabel that she would need to come to the station for some questioning, as she had been part of it too. Mabel promised to be at the police station the next morning.

Once they had gone, Stinkabell flew out from behind the wall. She thought about everything that had happened, and a smile spread over her rosy little cheeks.

'Why are you smiling?' asked Dillon.

'We did it! It actually worked.' She was so happy and relieved that she started shaking all over, from the tip of her wings to her little hairy toes. She flew high into the air and swooped back down, landing on Dillon's shoulder. Dillon joined in, running around the yard in huge circles, both of them laughing and whooping with joy.

Stinkabell spotted Mabel standing in the corner of the yard, smiling at the two friends as they celebrated. She flew over.

'Thank you for your help, we couldn't have done this without you,' she said, hovering above her.

'I'm so happy to have helped,' said Mabel, holding her hand out for Stinkabell. 'But I should have done something sooner... I'm so ashamed.'

'You saved us all,' said Stinkabell, 'and we've found a way to stop the Bogsnufflers, so from now all the bog creatures will be safe. We've saved the Land on the Other Side of the Pillow!'

'Come with me,' said Mabel, leading the way inside the dentist surgery and opening the door to a large cupboard. The cupboard was filled with jam jars, and inside each jar was a little Bog Fairy, flapping their wings or banging against the glass. Stinkabell scanned the rows of jars; she couldn't believe all these fairies had been here the whole time.

'We've got to get them out!' said Stinkabell. So Mabel and Dillon set to work, unscrewing the jar lids and releasing the fairies inside. Stinkabell flew up and down the shelves, looking into the jars. She got to a dark corner of the shelf — and suddenly she saw them. They were in two jars next to each other, both of the Bog Fairies' faces pressed to the side, grinning at her from behind the glass.

'Dillon—' squealed Stinkabell, above the noise of the other fairies, '—help me! It's my Mum and Dad!'

Dillon grabbed hold of the jars Stinkabell was pointing at and freed first her mum, then her dad. They zoomed out of the jars and surrounded Stinkabell in a giant hug.

Stinkabell could hardly believe it. Her parents were alive, and they were right here. Their wings all clapped together with joy.

CHAPTER 11
THE RETURN

Stinkabell, her parents and all the rescued Bog Fairies travelled back to the Land on the Other Side of the Pillow that same night. The whole bog was buzzing for weeks, with stories of how Stinkabell and her friend Dillon had saved them all.

The Bog Fairies all worked hard to rebuild their little tooth village. They were able to build brand-new houses for everyone, using the teeth from McAvity's jar, which Mabel had given them to take home.

As for McAvity, she was sentenced to five years' community service, and could often be spotted in a bright yellow jacket, picking litter up around the town. This was much to the delight of the children whose teeth she had stolen, who saved up their sweet and crisp packets and dropped them "accidently", every time they passed her.

Mabel was banned from working as a dental nurse, but she didn't mind. She took over the dentist surgery and set up her own doggy dentist, called "Canines". It was a tooth cleaning service strictly for dogs (which had been her real passion all along).

The fairies took home a big pot of the magic lava potion, and any time a Bogsnuffler came sniffing around, it was met with a rather unpleasant surprise! All the creatures in the bog were finally able to enjoy their lives, without fear of being gobbled up. The bog became a truly happy place to live.

Dillon sat up in bed on the night of the rescue and couldn't quite believe what he'd seen. He knew there was no point in trying to tell his mum or even his friends; they would just think he was crazy. Anyway, he'd promised Stinkabell that he would never reveal the secrets he'd learned about the Land on the Other Side of the Pillow.

But from time to time, Dillon smiles a secret smile, knowing that it wasn't all a dream.

And how does he know?

Because now she has passed her Tooth Taking Test, Stinkabell often drops in to share a biscuit or two…

THE END

About the Author

As a child, Hannah loved to read fantasy stories, especially those about far away magical lands which really captured her imagination. As an adult, she lives with her own family in Great Missenden, where Roald Dahl lived and worked, which further inspired her to write her own children's adventure story about a magical faraway place – the Land on the Other Side of the Pillow.

Acknowledgements

I would like to thank my husband, David, and all my family for their ideas and support, especially my Dad, James, who spent a lot of time helping me with early edits. A huge amount of thanks to David Millington, who provided the amazing illustrations for me, for bearing with me, and for your many hours of hard work.